Life in Kenya

Maryellen Burgess

Infomax Readers

Rosen Classroom™

New York

Published in 2013 by The Rosen Publishing Group, Inc.
29 East 21st Street, New York, NY 10010

Book Design: Katelyn Londino

Photo Credits: Cover Dmussman/Shutterstock.com; p. 4 meunierd/Shutterstock.com; pp. 5, 22 (lake, ocean) Antenna International/Shutterstock.com; pp. 6, 22 (desert) Piotr Gatlikv/Shutterstock.com; pp. 6, 22 (mountain) Comstock/Thinkstock.com; pp. 7, 22 (farm) © iStockphoto.com/WLDavies; p. 8 © iStockphoto.com/SimplyCreativePhotography; p. 9 Galyna Andrushko/Shutterstock.com; p. 10 Natalia Lysenko/Shutterstock.com; p. 11 Tom Cockrem/Photolibrary/Getty Images; pp. 12, 16 SIMON MAINA/Stringer/AFP/Getty Images; p. 13 EyesWideOpen/Contributor/Getty Images News/Getty Images; p. 14 Oli Scarff/Staff/Getty Images News/Getty Images; p. 15 Uriel Sinai/Stringer/Getty Images News/Getty Images; p. 17 Julian Finney/Staff/Getty Images Sport/Getty Images; p. 18 Cucumber Images/Shutterstock.com; pp. 19, 22 (park) marcokenya/Shutterstock.com; p. 20 InnaFelker/Shutterstock.com; p. 21 Geir Olav Lyngfjell/Shutterstock.com.

ISBN: 978-1-4488-9022-4
6-pack ISBN: 978-1-4488-9023-1

Manufactured in the United States of America

CPSIA Compliance Information: Batch #WS12RC: For further information contact Rosen Publishing, New York, New York at 1-800-237-9932.

Word Count: 393

Contents

Where Is Kenya?

Kenya is a country in Africa. It's a country with wild animals and many kinds of people. The people who live there are called Kenyans.

Kenya is in a part of Africa called east Africa. It's next to the Indian Ocean. There are big lakes in Kenya, too.

Deserts and Mountains

The land doesn't look the same all over Kenya. There are dry deserts in the north. You can see tall **mountains** there, too.

On the Farm

The land is very important to Kenyans. Most of them are farmers. They grow **crops** for their families to eat. They sell some crops, too.

Farmers in Kenya grow corn and wheat. They use these crops to make food. Some farmers also raise cows and goats.

Farmers in Kenya grow flowers, too. They sell the flowers to people in other countries. They also sell tea. Many people like to drink tea.

City Life

Some Kenyans live in cities. Nairobi is the biggest city in Kenya. There are many tall buildings in Nairobi.

Learning Is Important

Many Kenyans can speak two **languages**. They speak a language called Swahili and English. Some people speak other languages, too.

Learning is very important in Kenya. Children go to school. Many children walk to their schools.

Helping at Home

Children in Kenya also work hard to help their families. They help on their farms and do **chores** around the house.

One chore is getting water from a well. People in Kenya drink water from wells. They also use it to wash their hands and take baths.

Time to Eat!

Kenyans eat corn from their farms and fish that they catch. They also eat lots of rice. They cook on fires made with wood.

Sports in Kenya

People like to play sports in Kenya. They like to play soccer the most. Children in Kenya play soccer together after school.

People also play other sports in Kenya. They like to play basketball. Good runners come from Kenya, too.

Kenya's Wild Animals

Many wild animals live in Kenya. Elephants live there. You can see lions, zebras, and hippos in Kenya, too!

Many wild animals that live in Kenya stay in big parks. These parks keep them safe. People can see the wild animals in these parks.

People from all over the world travel to Kenya.

They come to see the wild animals that live there.

They go on **safaris** to see these animals.

A Different Kind of Life

How is life in Kenya like life where you live?

How is it different?

Nature in Kenya

Kenya has...

deserts

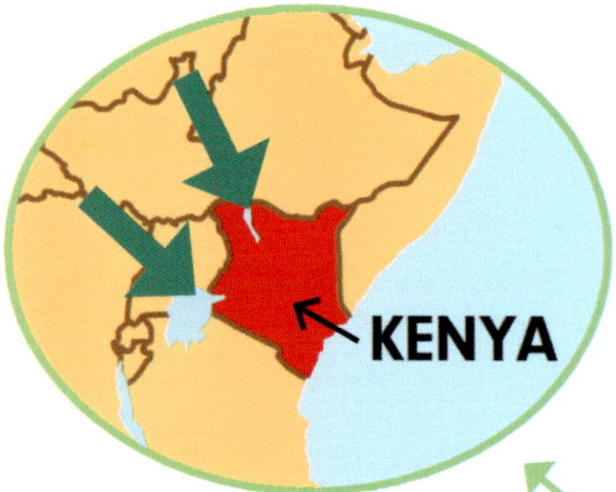

lakes

parks

farms

an ocean

mountains

Glossary

chore (CHOHR) A job done every day at home or on a farm.

crop (KRAHP) A plant grown on a farm.

language (LAYN-gwij) The way a person writes and speaks.

mountain (MOWN-tuhn) A very tall hill.

safari (suh-FAHR-ee) A trip to see wild animals.

Index